Do You Speak Fish?

written by **DJ CORCHIN**   illustrated by **DAN DOUGHERTY**

A boy ran into a fish.
He said, **"HELLO, FISH."**

But the fish
didn't reply.

"Hellooooo? Hey Fish, I'm **TALKING** to you!"

But the fish just looked at him.

"HOW RUDE," the boy said
and walked away.

The boy ran into a lion. He said, **"HELLO, LION."**

But the lion just ignored him.

"HEY LION! DON'T BE RUDE. I'M TALKING TO YOU!" the boy screamed.

That was a bad idea.

The boy ran into a bee.
He said, **"HELLO, BEE."**

The bee didn't say anything.

The boy threw his hands in the air and yelled,
"WHAT'S YOUR PROBLEM, BEE?!"

That was a bad idea too.

The boy came across a tree.
"HELLO THERE,"
the tree said.

The boy was surprised.

He didn't expect the tree
to say anything.

"Did you just say **HELLO?**" the boy asked.

"It would be rude not to," said the tree.

"I agree! This fish I talked to was very rude. She just ignored me."

"Well, do you speak Fish?" the tree asked.

"Why would I speak Fish? I'm a kid."

"Why would the fish speak Kid? She's a fish," the tree said.

"Everyone should speak Kid. That's the way it is."

"Not for a fish," the tree explained.

"But wait, I understand **YOU!**" the boy pointed out.

"I learned to speak Kid from a frog," the tree replied.

"Well, I don't speak Fish," the boy grumbled.

"I can teach you," the tree offered.

"You speak Fish too?"

"A carrot taught me," the tree replied.

"KIDDING! I'M KIDDING!" the tree laughed.

"Everyone knows carrots can't talk."

So the tree taught the boy to speak Fish.

The boy went back to the fish and said,
"HELLO, FISH!"

Except this time it sounded more like

The fish smiled and said,

BLURP

BLIP

BLURP

Suddenly the fish didn't seem so rude. "Well thank you. It **IS** a nice day out!" the boy replied back.

BLURP
BLURP

("So long!")

The boy went back to the lion.

ROOOAAR!!!
GRROWWL!
GRRRRR!!

The lion looked at him, confused.

Then he burst out laughing so hard
that he fell backwards with his legs in the air.

The boy looked puzzled.

He wasn't sure if what he said came out right.
Maybe it was better he didn't know.

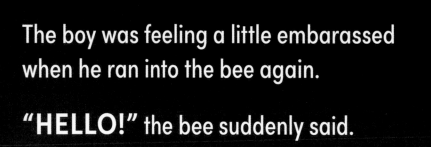

The boy was feeling a little embarassed
when he ran into the bee again.

"HELLO!" the bee suddenly said.
Stunned, the boy replied, "Um, hello. You speak Kid?"

"A little bit. A fish just taught me. She said a boy was kind enough
to learn Fish, so she thought she should try to learn to speak Kid.
A tree taught her."

That made the boy happy.

From then on, the boy, the bee, the fish, and the lion
would sit by the tree each day and share stories.

Sometimes they would speak Kid.
Sometimes they would speak Fish, or Bee, or Lion.
They always worked to understand each other...

and their world got a whole lot bigger.

To Alfie

Text © 2017, 2021 by The phazelFOZ Company, LLC • Illustrations © 2021 by Dan Dougherty
Cover and internal design © 2021 by Sourcebooks • Sourcebooks and the colophon are registered trademarks
of Sourcebooks. • All rights reserved. • The characters and events portrayed in this book are fictitious or are used
fictitiously. Any similarity to real persons, living or dead, is purely coincidental and not intended by the author.
Procreate and Photoshop were used to prepare the full color art. • Published by Sourcebooks eXplore, an imprint of
Sourcebooks Kids • P.O. Box 4410, Naperville, Illinois 60567-4410 • (630) 961-3900
sourcebookskids.com • Library of Congress Cataloging-in-Publication Data is on file with the publisher.
Source of Production: 1010 Printing Asia Limited, North Point, Hong Kong, China
Date of Production: June 2021 • Run Number: 5021999 • Printed and bound in China. • OGP 10 9 8 7 6 5 4 3 2 1

"Did you know the boy once told me his feet smell worse than **HIPPOPOTAMUS BREATH?**"